I Like to Read® books, created by award-winning picture book artists as well as talented newcomers, instill confidence and the joy of reading in new readers.

We want to hear every new reader say, "I like to read!"

Visit our website for flash cards, activities, and more about the series:
www.holidayhouse.com/ILiketoRead
#ILTR

This book has been officially leveled by using the
F&P Text Level Gradient™ Leveling System.

For Tedd and Carol, who love cats and who take the cake
in the generous hearts category
—M.H. & M.W.

I LIKE TO READ is a registered trademark of Holiday House Publishing, Inc.

Text copyright © 2022 by Martha Hamilton and Mitch Weiss
Illustrations copyright © 2022 by Steve Henry
All Rights Reserved
HOLIDAY HOUSE is registered in the U.S. Patent and Trademark Office.
Printed and bound in September 2021 at C&C Offset, Shenzhen, China.
The artwork was created with ink, watercolor, and acrylic paint on 300 lb. watercolor paper.
www.holidayhouse.com
First Edition
1 3 5 7 9 10 8 6 4 2

This book has been officially leveled by using the
F&P Text Level Gradient™ Leveling System.

Library of Congress Cataloging-in-Publication Data

Names: Hamilton, Martha, author. | Weiss, Mitch, 1951- author. | Henry, Steve, 1948- illustrator.
Title: The cats and the cake / by Martha Hamilton and Mitch Weiss ; illustrated by Steve Henry.
Other titles: I like to read (New York, N.Y.)
Description: First edition. | New York : Holiday House, 2022. | Series: I like to read | Audience: Ages 4-8. | Audience: Grades K-1.
Summary: Two cats fight over a cake, but ultimately learn the value of sharing.
Identifiers: LCCN 2021013733 | ISBN 9780823447565 (hardcover)
Subjects: LCSH: Cats—Juvenile fiction. | Cake—Juvenile fiction.
Sharing—Juvenile fiction. | Humorous stories. | CYAC: Cats—Fiction.
Cake—Fiction. | Sharing—Fiction. | Humorous stories. | LCGFT: Humorous fiction.
Readers (Publications) Classification: LCC PZ7.H182637 Cat 2022 | DDC [E]—dc23
LC record available at https://lccn.loc.gov/2021013733

ISBN 978-0-8234-4756-5 (hardcover)

The Cats and the Cake

by **Martha Hamilton**
and **Mitch Weiss**

Pictures by **Steve Henry**

I Like to Read®

HOLIDAY HOUSE • NEW YORK